The Grumpy Little Girls and the Bouncy Ferret

Maisie

BESTEST FRIEND: Lulu

PETS: Only the Blob – (my baby brother!)

FAVOURITE GAME: Let's Pretend!

YUMMIEST FOOD: Slimy worms (Spaghetti, silly!)

SCARIEST SCARY THING: Spiders. Eeeek!

GETS GRUMPY: When Lulu won't play Let's Pretend...

FIZ

REAL NAME: Felicity. Yurgh!

BESTEST THING: Bouncing on my trampoline

WANTS V V V V MUCH: To learn to do a proper cartwheel

HATES: Playing quietly indoors

GETS GRUMPY: When my big brothers sit on me...

Ruby

favourite Cat

LOVES: Horse riding and karate lessons

HATES: Piano lessons. Snore!

WANTS V V V V MUCH: A pony and pierced ears. (But mum says I've got to wait till I'm 12!)

FAVOURITE COLOUR: Pink, pink, pink!

GETS GRUMPY: When Maisie and Lulu and Fiz won't do what I tell them...

LULU

BESTEST FRIEND: Maisie. (Or Warren, my woodlouse.)

PETS: 3 cats, 12 fish, 2 guinea pigs, 4 Giant Amazonian snails, 1 rabbit, 1 rat, 1 woodlouse

WANTS V V V MUCH: A ferret!

YUKKIEST FOOD: Meat

GETS GRUMPY: When mum makes me clean out my pets' cages...

First published in Great Britain by HarperCollins*Publishers* Ltd in 2000

1 3 5 7 9 10 8 6 4 2

ISBN: 0 00 664770 7

Concept copyright © Arroyo Projects 2000

Text and characters copyright © Lindsay Camp 2000

Illustrations copyright © Daniel Postgate 2000

The author and illustrator assert the moral right to be identified
as the author and illustrator of the work.

The HarperCollins website address is:
www.**fire**and**water**.com

Printed and bound in Singapore.

The Grumpy Little Girls and the Bouncy Ferret

Lindsay Camp and Daniel Postgate

An imprint of HarperCollinsPublishers

There was one thing Lulu wanted
more than anything else in all the world.
She already had one rat, one rabbit, two guinea pigs,
three cats, four Giant Amazonian snails and 12 fish.
Oh yes, and a woodlouse called Warren.

Now she was desperate for a ferret. But she knew what her mum and dad would say.

Her mum would say, "You've got enough animals already."

And her dad would say, "You don't look after them properly. How long is it since you cleaned out that poor rabbit's hutch?"

So on Saturday morning, Lulu cleaned out Rex's hutch.

*T*hen, at lunchtime, she said to her mum and dad, very quickly, "Can I have a ferret? It's ages since I had any new animals."

"You don't look after the ones you've got," said her dad. "How long is it since you cleaned –"

"This morning," Lulu cut him off. "I cleaned out Rex's hutch this morning."

Her mum and dad looked at each other.

"Aren't ferrets rather fierce and bitey?" asked her mum.

"No," said Lulu. "I saw one on TV and it slept in the man's bed, under his pillow. So can I? Please, please, **please**!"

"No!" said her mum and dad, together.

And then her mum said, more kindly,
"Maybe for your birthday, Lulu. But not now.
A ferret would be much too expensive."

But it was years and years until Lulu's birthday,
and she wanted a ferret now.

"It's not fair!" she said, very grumpily indeed.

She was still quite grumpy after lunch when her dad offered to take her to the park, where there was an excellent new climbing frame.

But she cheered up when they arrived and found Maisie and Ruby already playing on it.

"It's a spaceship," explained Maisie. "And those are evil aliens who aren't allowed to come on board," she went on, pointing to some little boys.

When they got tired of that game, they sat on the grass in the sunshine, and Lulu told Maisie and Ruby about how much she wanted a ferret, and how her mum and dad said it was too expensive.

"You could save up," said Ruby.

"But I only get 50p a week," groaned Lulu. "It would take ages."

"I know what we could do," said Maisie, who didn't like to see her best friend looking miserable. "We could steal lots of money from a bank. We'd need a big sack to put all the money in, and masks to cover up our faces."

Lulu laughed.

"I think that's a silly idea," said Ruby. "How would we get to the bank, anyway? We'd have to ask one of our mums to take us...

"...and then they'd want to know why, and we'd get into trouble."

aisie looked grumpy. "I bet you can't think of a better idea," she said.

"I can," said Ruby. "We could open a shop, and sell things that we make."

Lulu and Maisie stared at her with their mouths open. It wasn't a good idea. It was a brilliant one.

"Come on," said Lulu excitedly. "Let's go back to my house, so we can start our shop straight away."

But when they got back to Lulu's house, the shop didn't seem quite such a brilliant idea after all.

To start with, they couldn't agree what to call it. Ruby said she'd thought of it, so it should be called Ruby's Superstore.

But Lulu and Maisie didn't like that name.

Then they argued about what the shop should sell. So, in the end, they had to open three shops.

3p

Magic
Biscuits

Lulu's
Gallery

9p

6p

8p

Ruby's
Scent

Lulu lived in a quiet road, so they didn't have many customers. In fact, they didn't have any except Lulu's mum, who bought something from each shop. After a while, they got bored.

"We're never going to get enough money for a ferret like this," wailed Lulu.

Just then, Lulu's mum called out, "Lulu, Fiz is on the phone!"

Fiz sounded very excited, and rather out of breath.

"You'll never guess what I'm doing," she panted.

"What?" said Lulu.

"Not telling," gasped Fiz. "You'll have to come and see."

So Lulu's dad gave the girls a lift to Fiz's house.
And there in the garden, they saw it.

"It's fantastic!" said Ruby.

"It's totally wicked," said Fiz, whose big brothers were always saying that kind of thing. "I could go on bouncing all day. But you can have a go."

Ruby and Maisie each had a turn on the trampoline. Lulu watched them, feeling rather miserable about her ferret.

"Go on, Lulu," said Maisie, climbing off. "It's brilliant!"

So Lulu climbed on to the trampoline and started to bounce, quite little bounces to begin with, then higher and higher ones.

And as she bounced, she started to feel better – as if, well, as if everything was going to be all right.

At bedtime, Lulu said to her mum, "Mum, remember when you went on that long walk, and everybody gave you lots of money?"

"Yes," said her mum. "My sponsored walk."

"Does it have to be a walk?" asked Lulu. "Could it be a sponsored something else?"

"I suppose it could," said Mum, looking puzzled. "As long as the money went to a good cause."

"Oh yes, it will," said Lulu.

"What are you planning?"

"Nothing, Mum," said Lulu, closing her eyes.

But two weeks later, on a sunny Saturday, Lulu, Maisie, Ruby and Fiz held their Grand Sponsored Bounce.

Each of them was going to bounce in turn, until they'd bounced all morning.

Half the money, the girls had agreed with their parents, was going to the RSPCA, to help look after sick and lost animals.

The other half? Well, Lulu's mum and dad had a pretty good idea...

...how Lulu was planning to spend it.

Ruby

LOVES: Horse riding and karate lessons

HATES: Piano lessons. Snore!

WANTS V V V V MUCH: A pony and pierced ears. (But mum says I've got to wait till I'm 12!)

FAVOURITE COLOUR: Pink, pink, pink!

GETS GRUMPY: When Maisie and Lulu and Fiz won't do what I tell them...

favourite Cat

LULU

BESTEST FRIEND: Maisie. (Or Warren, my woodlouse.)

PETS: 3 cats, 12 fish, 2 guinea pigs, 4 Giant Amazonian snails, 1 rabbit, 1 rat, 1 woodlouse

WANTS V V V MUCH: A ferret!

YUKKIEST FOOD: Meat

GETS GRUMPY: When mum makes me clean out my pets' cages...

Have you read all the stories about us?

The Grumpy Little Girls and the Princess Party
ISBN 0 00 664708 1

The Grumpy Little Girls and the Wobbly Sleepover
ISBN 0 00 664709 X

The Grumpy Little Girls and the Bouncy Ferret
ISBN 0 00 664770 7

The Grumpy Little Girls and the Naughty Little Boy
ISBN 0 00 664769 3